WELCOME BACK, PUFFIN!

by Dawn Bentley

Illustrated by Beth Stover

For Aidan Nicholas Bentley, who wanted me to dedicate the "puppy" book to him. I love you so much! — D.B.

Published by Soundprints Division of Trudy Corporation, Norwalk, Connecticut.

Book design: Marcin D. Pilchowski
Editor: Laura Gates Galvin
Editorial assistance: Chelsea Shriver

First Edition 2003
10 9 8 7 6 5 4 3 2 1
Printed in China

Acknowledgments:
Our very special thanks to Dr. Gary R. Graves of the Department of Systematic Biology at the Smithsonian Institution's National Museum of Natural History for his curatorial review.
Soundprints would also like to thank Ellen Nanney and Robyn Bissette at the Smithsonian Institution's Office of Product Development and Licensing for their help in the creation of this book.
Many thanks to Laura Gates Galvin, my editor-extraordinaire, who made this project a joy to work on! (D.B.)

Library of Congress Cataloging-in-Publication Data

Bentley, Dawn.
    Welcome back, Puffin! / Dawn Bentley ; illustrated by Beth Stover.
       p. cm.
    Summary: Puffin and her mate fly over the ocean to an island where, each year, they have a baby in the very same burrow.
    ISBN 1-59249-009-3 (pbk.)
    1. Puffins—Juvenile fiction. [1. Puffins—Fiction.] I. Stover, Beth, 1969- ill. II. Title.

PZ10.3.B4517 We 2003
[E]—dc21

                                                                2002191152

Table of Contents

A note to the reader:
Throughout this story you will see words in **bold letters**. There is more information about these words in the glossary. The glossary is in the back of the book.

Chapter 1
Puffin Is Back!

Far from a
cold beach, a
puffin flies over
the ocean to
an **island**.

Puffin spends most
of her life at sea.
Puffin flies to the
island once a year
to have a baby.

Puffin looks clumsy when she flies. Her body is big. Her wings are small.

Puffin tips and wobbles and makes a rough landing. Puffin swims better than she flies!

Puffin finds the same **burrow** she uses every year. The burrow is a long, dark tunnel.

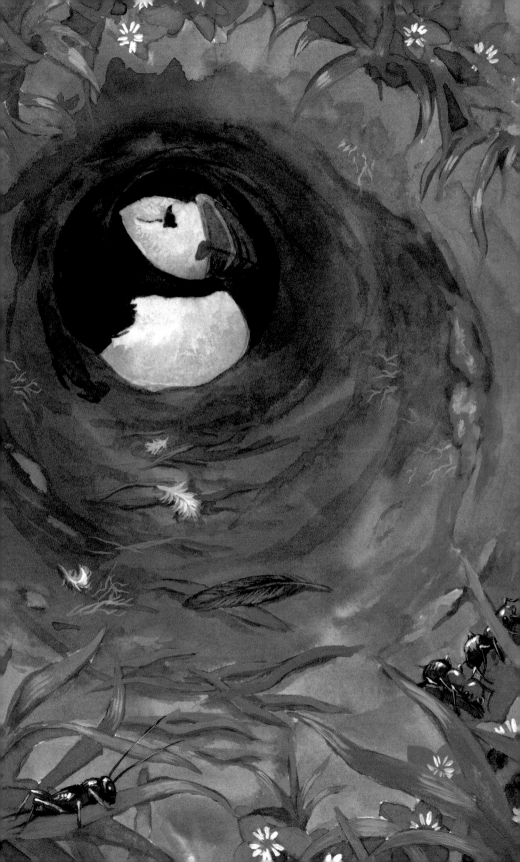

Chapter 2
Puffin's Egg

There is a small nest at the end of the tunnel. This is where Puffin lays her egg.

Puffin and her **mate** do not sit on their egg like other birds. They tuck the egg close to their bodies. They cover the egg with a wing to keep it warm.

More than a month later, a baby puffin pecks his way out of the eggshell.

Baby Puffin is not colorful like his parents. He is covered with fluffy, gray feathers.

Chapter 3

Welcome, Baby Puffin

Baby Puffin is hungry! Feeding the baby is a big job for Puffin and her mate.

Puffin finds small fish for Baby Puffin to eat. Sometimes Baby Puffin eats ten times a day!

Now, Baby Puffin is almost two months old. He has eaten nearly two thousand fish!

Chapter 4

Fly Home, Puffin!

The weather turns cool. Puffin's bright colors begin to fade. The white feathers on her head turn gray. Her bright orange legs turn dark.

It is time for Puffin and her mate to return to sea. It is time for Baby Puffin to be on his own.

Puffin jumps off the cliff. She flaps her wings. She begins her journey out to sea.

Baby Puffin rests in the burrow. His wing feathers are fully grown. He is ready to leave the island, too.

Baby Puffin runs off the edge of the cliff. He flaps his wings fast. He splashes into the water.

Baby Puffin will need to practice flying. He feels right at home in the water. Other young puffins join him.

Baby Puffin quickly learns how to find fish. Soon he will travel out to sea, just like Puffin.

Glossary

Burrow: a hole in which an animal lives or hides.

Island: land completely surrounded by water.

Mate: one of a pair of animals that breeds to have babies.

Wilderness Facts
About the Atlantic Puffin

Puffins spend more time in the water than in the air. North Atlantic puffins live in the oceans between Maine, Canada, Greenland, Iceland, Norway, Ireland and Great Britain. Each spring, puffins return to the islands where they were hatched.

Puffins can keep their eyes open
underwater. They have clear eyelids
that cover their eyes and protect
them. Puffins also have a special
bill. Ridges on the bill help Puffins
hold fish in place. When they open
their bills to catch another fish, they
don't lose the first one!

In the winter, puffins' beaks are small and not brightly colored. They also lose the bright white feathers on their face. Gray feathers replace them. During this time, they shed their wing feathers and then grow new ones. They cannot fly until the new feathers grow in.

Animals that live near puffins on the nesting islands off the coast of Maine include:

Great black-backed gulls

Herring gulls

Harbor seals